How Six Little Ipu Got Their Names

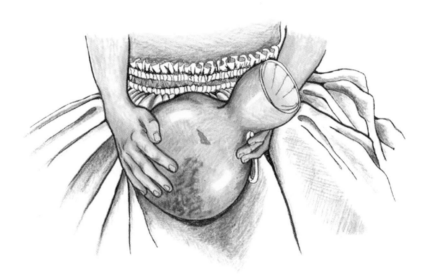

Debi Brimmer and Julie Coleson

Illustrated by Julie Coleson

 BESS PRESS

3565 Harding Avenue
Honolulu, Hawai'i 96816
phone: (808) 734-7159
fax: (808) 732-3627
e-mail: sales@besspress.com
http://www.besspress.com

This book is dedicated with much *aloha* to the students of
Hula Me Ka Puʻuwai, of Rockville, Maryland,
who inspired this story.

Design: Carol Colbath

Library of Congress Cataloging-in-Publication Data

Brimmer, Debi.
How six little ipu got their names /
Debi Brimmer and Julie Coleson ;
illustrated by Julie Coleson.
p. cm.
Includes illustrations, glossary.
ISBN 1-57306-186-7
1. Gourds - Hawaii - Juvenile fiction.
2. Hula (Dance) - Juvenile fiction.
3. Musical instruments - Hawaii -
Juvenile fiction. I. Coleson, Julie.
II. Title.
PZ7.B75 2005   398-dc21

09 08 07 06 05   5 4 3 2 1

Printed through Colorcraft Ltd. in Hong Kong

CD recorded at Rendez-Vous Recording
Performer: Kahale Richardson-Naki
Production coordinator: Caryl Nishioka

Cover art depicts Hula Supply Center, established 1946.

Once upon a time, in the islands of Hawai'i, on a patch of ground tangled with vines, six little bottle gourds opened their eyes for the very first time. As they looked about, they could see the emerald green slopes of their valley reaching up toward the sky, hear the singing of the birds, and smell the sweet earth from which they grew.

For what seemed like a very long time, the little gourds slept peacefully, drank the soft rainwater that sank into the earth around them, enjoyed the tickle of the wind and the warmth of the sun.

"Ah, what a wonderful home we have," said one of the little gourds.

"Yes, we are so lucky to live here," said another.

"I hope we never have to leave it," exclaimed the smallest.

Every few days, a farmer would come by to see how the little gourds were growing. Sometimes he would turn them this way and that, and when any of them were growing so large that they almost touched the ground, he would fasten their vines a little higher, to keep them from falling onto the moist earth.

"We no like rotten spots on you, eh?" he would say.

The farmer always carried a large water gourd that held his drinking water. Sometimes, if the water gourd wasn't too busy, he would tell the little gourds stories about growing up in this very same gourd patch.

Once, the smallest gourd asked what was beyond their emerald valley. But having lived in this spot all his life, the water gourd replied, "Oh, just other vines and other farmers. Nothing to get excited about."

One bright sunny day, the farmer came into the patch with a huge cart. It was filled with wooden baskets. The little gourds began to chatter among themselves, wondering why the farmer had brought the cart. Suddenly, the largest of the little gourds felt himself being lifted up in the farmer's hands.

SNAP!

"My vine is broken! My vine is broken!" he cried, as the farmer set him in one of the baskets. Before any of the other gourds knew what had happened, they too were broken from their vines and set into the basket. Such a clattering of voices came from the little gourds.

"My vine is broken too!"

"Oh, dear, where are we going?"

"I'm so afraid!"

"I think I'm going to be siiiiick!"

Soon, the farmer finished his labor and pulled the cart out of the gourd patch.

The walls of the basket were too high for the little gourds to see much other than the blue sky above them. The gentle movement of the cart as it made its way through the gourd patch lulled them all to sleep. They awoke when they were loaded into the back of a truck. As the truck made its way down the valley road, their basket bounced up and down and slid from side to side. The little gourds shouted,

"Hold on!"

"Oh no!"

"I want to go home!"

"I think I'm going to be siiiiick!"

As the sun sank lower into the sky, the truck finally stopped. "Thank goodness," said the largest gourd, "we are back home at last! I can't wait to connect to my vine again."

4

But as the driver lowered the back of the truck and placed
the baskets on the ground, the little gourds began to see that they were
not in their beloved gourd patch at all.

This was a strange place with a little house in front and a big workshop in
the back. As the baskets were carried into the workshop, the little gourds
could see that they were not alone. There were gourds hanging in nets from
the ceiling, gourds in great wooden boxes on the floor, and gourds lined up
all the way down a long, wooden workbench.

As soon as the little gourds saw the others, they started to chatter.

"Hello! Who are you?"

"Where are we?"

"What's going to happen to us?"

And of course, when so many folks are talking at
the same time, no one can hear anything. Soon, the
little gourds were hung up in their own net, right next
to the others.

As soon as they were left alone, they whispered among themselves and decided that the largest of them would ask all the questions. "Excuse me, but where are we?" he asked.

From the top of the workbench came a booming voice. "You are in 'Ioane's workshop, little ones. Someday you will be made into *ipu hula* for dancers. My name is Ka Leo Kilakila, and I am an *ipu heke*. I sing for the *hula*. You may call me Uncle Ka Leo. You are very lucky. 'Ioane is a fine and famous craftsman! His *hula* implements sing all over the wide world!"

"An *ipu hula*? Me?" said the smallest gourd, without any idea what that meant.

"Yes," answered Uncle Ka Leo with a yawn, "even the smallest gourds have singing voices. You'll see. For now, just be content and sleep. It may be some time before you find your voices and your new vines."

Then Ka Leo Kilakila himself went to sleep on the workbench.

Well, you can imagine the conversations that went on from there.

"New vines?"

"Voices?"

"What does that mean?"

"What is an instrument?"

"Will we be together?"

"I want to go home!"

"I think I'm going to be siiiiick!"

Soon, they were all moved just outside the workshop, into a sunny patch of sandy, dry land. Many days passed while the little gourds did nothing much, other than sleep and wonder what was going to happen to them. Their skins changed from soft and green to hard and brown. And they got very, very thirsty.

"Where is the rain?" asked the smallest. "I am so dry, I can feel my seeds starting to rattle."

"Don't worry," said Uncle Ka Leo through the open window. "You will feel thirsty for only a little while more."

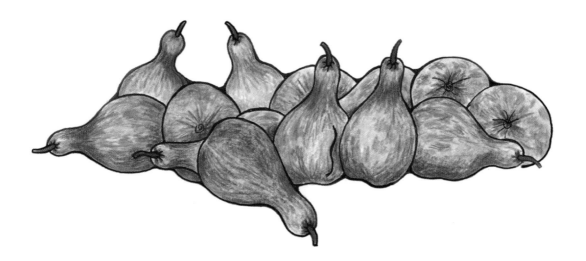

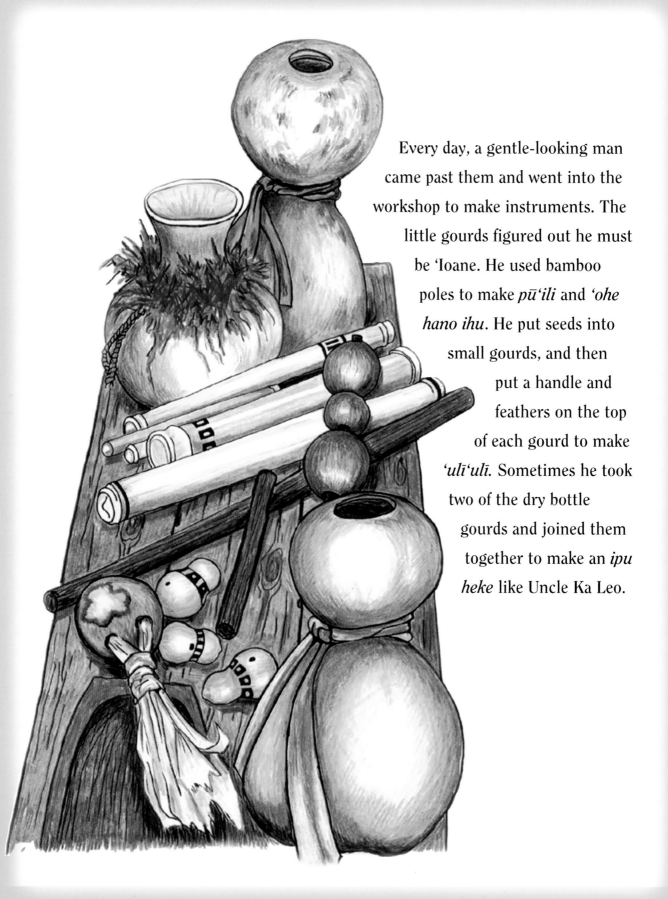

Every day, a gentle-looking man came past them and went into the workshop to make instruments. The little gourds figured out he must be 'Ioane. He used bamboo poles to make *pū'ili* and *'ohe hano ihu*. He put seeds into small gourds, and then put a handle and feathers on the top of each gourd to make *'ulī'ulī*. Sometimes he took two of the dry bottle gourds and joined them together to make an *ipu heke* like Uncle Ka Leo.

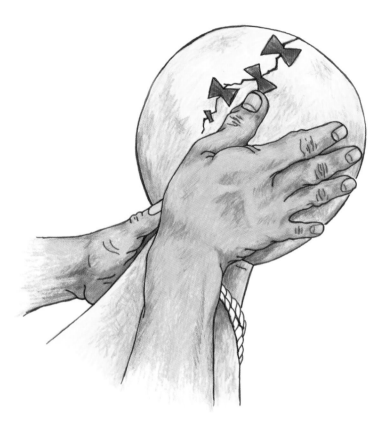

Uncle Ka Leo himself had a nasty crack down his forehead, but 'Ioane fixed it with several small butterfly patches. Uncle sighed in contentment, feeling more like his old self again.

'Ioane picked him up and said, "K-den, let's hear your voice now, Uncle."

'Ioane took the big *ipu heke* into one hand and began to tap on its tummy with the other, first with the bottom of his palm, and then with his fingers. The little gourds were amazed, for out of Uncle's mouth came a deep, powerful, and beautiful voice.

'Ioane began to chant, and the two of them sang together about the beauties of the very same emerald valley where the little gourds had been born.

When ʻIoane finished the chant, he placed Uncle back on the workbench and left the workroom for the day.

The little gourds were so excited. "Oh, Uncle, you mean WE will sing like that? Us?"

Uncle Ka Leo chuckled to himself and said, "No, my little ones. Only an *ipu heke* like me can call the song. Your job will be to answer back and help the *hula* dancers time their steps."

ʻIoane came back into the workshop, lifted Uncle off the workbench, and put him into a box. "Well, it seems I am going home now, my little ones," Ka Leo said. "Be good, be strong, sing well and true, and someday you will find your new vines.

Aloha!"

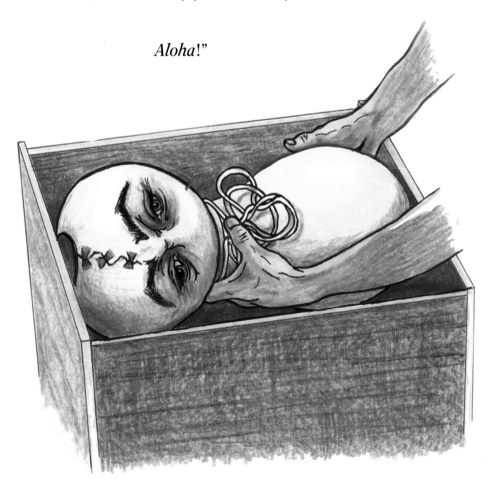

"Wow! I don't think I will mind being away from home if we get to make such beautiful music," said the largest gourd.

"Me either," said several of the others.

But one of the gourds, who had a bit of a dent in his side, looked very worried. "What about me?" he said. "I have this dent from where I sat next to a stake too long. Will I still sing sweetly?"

But none of the other little gourds could answer him, because they just didn't know.

When the time came for the six little gourds to become *ipu*, 'Ioane brought them back into the workshop and put them on his worktable, one by one. He took a small saw and removed the tops of their necks, where they used to be connected to their vines. One after another, the little gourds felt a rush of warm air on their insides. They could breathe again!

Next, 'Ioane carefully cleaned each gourd inside. He removed the seeds and put them into a big jar. Later he would plant the seeds to grow new gourds. He scrubbed the gourds' outsides and coated them with sweet-smelling oil. He made a small hole in the side of each of their necks, slipped a white cord into it, and then set all six gourds on the drying shelf.

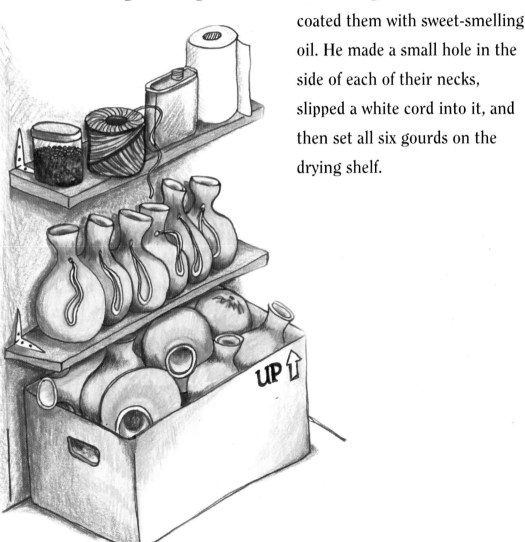

The very next day, all cleaned up and shiny, they were taken down from the shelf and put into a large wooden box. Up onto the back of the pickup truck they went again, but this time, they were not so frightened. So many wonderful new things had happened to them since they left their gourd patch.

"We are having such an adventure!" they exclaimed. "Where in the world can we be going now?"

When the truck stopped again, they were carried into a *hula* shop. Fantastic sights awaited the six little *ipu*: colorful *lei* made out of feathers and flowers and ribbons were hanging all over the walls. Many of the *hula* instruments that 'Ioane had made in his workshop were sitting on the store shelves. Other *ipu* that 'Ioane had made were sitting on a long shelf by the window.

'Ioane took the six little *ipu* and put them on the window shelf too.

"Hello! How are you? Nice to see you!" exclaimed the six little *ipu*. "Is this where we find our new vines?"

They spent the rest of the day chattering with their new friends and looking back at the

people who peered into the window of the *hula* shop.

A few days later, a young woman came over to the shelf and sat a large box beneath it. She looked over all the *ipu* and said, "I need six small *ipu* for the *keiki* class." She reached up and one by one took down five of the little *ipu* and put them into the box with lots of white puffy things.

"Oh, this tickles," gasped the largest of the little *ipu*.

But the little *ipu* with the dent in his side was left sitting on the shelf, and he cried, "Oh, I knew it! I will be left behind because I am not perfect! Oh dear, oh dear!"

But before any of the other *ipu* could say another word, the young woman reached for the dented *ipu* and placed it in the box beside the others.

"Phew, that was close!" said the dented *ipu*. "I thought I was going to be siiiiick!"

When all six were nestled in the box, the top was closed, and darkness was all the little *ipu* could see.

For many hours after that, they felt nothing but bumping, swaying, and more bumping. They lost all track of time, and they could not tell if they had been in the box for hours or days. Then, finally, "thump," the box was set down on the ground.

It was quiet outside the box for the longest time. Then they heard the sound of keys and the opening of a door. Their box was lifted and set carefully down again. The six little *ipu* heard sniffing noises from outside the box, first on one side and then the other. A woman laughed and scolded the sniffers gently, saying, "All right, puppy babies, no more, no more!"

Then their box was lifted once again and carried down some stairs into a cool place. For a long time, the six little *ipu* listened for voices and called, "Hello? Is anyone out there?" But the only sound they heard was the chirping of crickets. Soon, worn out by this last part of their great adventure, they fell fast asleep.

The next day, they awoke to the sound of seven girls' voices and the pounding of seven pairs of feet running down the stairs. A door burst open, and the little girls chattered and laughed all around them. Things settled down when a woman's voice told them to start their warm-up, and seven little voices began to chant *"'ekahi, 'elua,*

'ekolu, 'ehā, 'elima, 'eono, 'ehiku, 'ewalu, 'eiwa, 'umi" over and over again.

Soon, another woman, who turned out to be the *kumu*, came into the room and told the girls that their *ipu* had arrived at last. A great shout of "Hurray!" went up from the girls, and the air was full of their questions.

"Can we see them now?"

"What color is mine?"

"Oh, please, Auntie, can't we open the box?"

"Wait a minute," said Auntie Ka'ie. "First there are things you must know. These *ipu* have come a long way to be yours. They will become a part of your *hula* and need to be treated with respect. You must take care not to bump them into anything or drop them on the floor. They have a delicate spot on the bottom that you must never hit."

Auntie took her own *ipu* and showed the little girls exactly where the spot was. She showed them how she put her hand through the cord at its neck to help hold her *ipu*, and how she did the *pa'i* by using two places on her hand to make different sounds.

Meanwhile the six little *ipu* in the box were listening to Auntie too. This was more than they ever knew about themselves. In an excited whisper, the smallest *ipu* said to the others, "This must be where we find our voices and our new vines. This must be what Uncle Ka Leo was talking about!"
All the others agreed.

Then came the moment the little girls had been waiting for. Auntie opened the box. Seven excited little faces looked down into the box, and six little *ipu* looked up.

"Noelani, since you already have your own *ipu*, would you help me set these on the mat?" asked Auntie.

"Of course," said Noelani.

Auntie and Noelani took the little *ipu* out one by one, and to the *ipu*'s surprise, they heard a voice exclaim, "Oh my goodness! Oh, welcome! Welcome!"

The six little *ipu* looked toward the strange voice. To their surprise, they saw another little *ipu*, just like themselves.

"Where are we?" they asked fearfully. "What is this place?"

"Don't worry! These little girls are students of *hula*. This is their class. Oh! How exciting that now I will have brothers and sisters to sing with!"

"Now," said Auntie, "who gets hers first? Hmmmm, this smallest *ipu* looks just the right size for Lisa's hand."

Lisa was the youngest dancer in the class. Lisa placed her small hand around the neck of the smallest *ipu*. "Gee, it feels just right!" exclaimed Lisa, and she went back to her place on the mat.

Rebecca, Mattie, Malia, Laura, and Samantha each stepped up in turn to test the *ipu* and see which one fit their hands. One by one, the six little *ipu* found themselves nestled in the arms of one of the girls. Each time, Auntie asked, "Are you sure? Is this the *ipu* that is really, really yours?"

Well, each little *ipu* could have told the woman that all by themselves. From the moment the *ipu* were picked up, they felt something they hadn't felt since those first days in the sleepy warmth of the emerald valley. They felt wanted and connected and cared for.

"I don't miss my vine anymore! I wonder if this is what Uncle Ka Leo meant? Are these little girls our new vines?"

Before anyone could guess the answer, Auntie started talking again, and everyone, *ipu* and dancers alike, were all ears.

"Now, you will need to hold your *ipu* for a while and really get to know what it looks and sounds like. Let's practice holding them and do a few beats."

Auntie helped each girl slip her wrist through the cord of the *ipu* and begin to play. Pretty soon the room was filled with the sounds of *ipu* trying to sing.

The six little *ipu* were overjoyed. "We're singing! We're singing! We've found our voices!" they shouted.

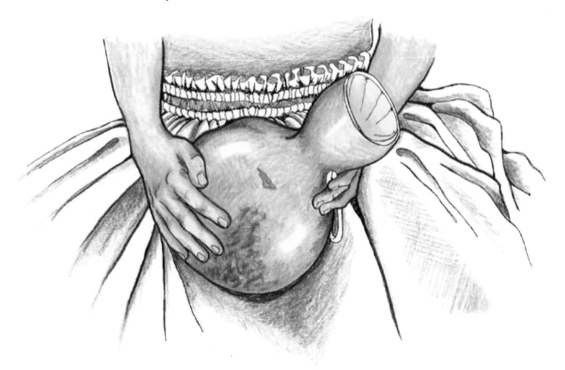

"Shush, little ladies, shush," said Auntie. "I will leave you for a few minutes so that you can get to know your *ipu*. Since your *ipu* is going to become a friend and a helper in your dancing, you might want to give it a name. So study your *ipu*, and a name might just come into your head before you leave today."

Auntie left the room, and once again the air filled with the sounds of *ipu* singing. Oh, it wasn't perfect singing like Uncle Ka Leo's, and they weren't all singing together, but they had indeed found their voices at last.

When Auntie returned, she began to teach the little girls a *hula,* using their *ipu*. They practiced very hard, and every time they had to stop, they couldn't wait to start again!

A few minutes before class was over, Auntie asked the girls if they had found names for their *ipu*.

Lisa spoke up first and said that her *ipu* was so pretty, she was going to call her "Nani."

Malia showed everyone the pretty dots on one side of her *ipu* and said that she was going to name her "Dottie."

Laura said "My *ipu* is Leo Akamai; I will listen for his wise voice to tell me how to step!"

Samantha named her *ipu* "Kiko," because she loved the little spot on his neck.

Rebecca decided not to name her *ipu* quite yet—she wanted to take him home and think of a name for him there.

Noelani's *ipu*, which had been with her for some time, was named "Lucky," because she felt very lucky that he was hers.

Mattie said, "Mine is named 'Mino'—look, there's a dent right here on his side."

Well, let me tell you, all the little *ipu* just held their breaths when they heard this, and looked at their little friend. They knew how sensitive he was about that dent!

But before any of them could say another word, Mattie spoke again. "But listen! This dent is where he sings the sweetest!"

Mino gasped and looked at his brothers and sisters. He exclaimed, "Look! Look! See my dent here? It is where I sing the sweetest!"

And all the little *ipu* laughed together in relief.

When class was over, the girls began to leave. Six little *ipu* snuggled down into the bottom of six *hula* bags, happy to have new names, new homes, and new adventures awaiting them.

Glossary

The mark that looks like an upside-down apostrophe is called an *'okina* (oh-KEE-nah). That is a place where your voice breaks, as when you say "uh-oh."

butterfly patches: butterfly-shaped pieces, called *pewa* (PEH vah) in Hawaiian, that are used to mend cracks in implements and containers.

'ehā (eh HAH): four.

'ehiku (eh HEE koo): seven.

'eiwa (eh EE vah): nine.

'ekahi (eh KAH hee): one.

'ekolu (eh KOH loo): three.

'elima (eh LEE mah): five.

'elua (eh LOO ah): two.

'eono (eh OH noh): six.

'ewalu (eh VAH loo): eight.

Hula Me Ka Pu'uwai (HOO lah meh kah POO oo vye): "Hula from the Heart."

'Ioane (ee oh AH neh): one who gives new life to gourds.

ipu (EE poo): a *hula* implement made from a cured and cleaned bottle gourd. The *ipu* is held in one hand and rhythmically struck with the palm and fingers of the other.

ipu heke (EE poo HEH keh): an implement made by joining two *ipu* together, one on top of the other. *Heke,* which means "greatest," describes the top gourd (and also the feathered top of the *'ulī'ulī*). *Ipu heke* are played by seated chanters to provide rhythm for the *hula* chant.

28

Ka'ie (kah EE eh): the *'ie* (or *'ie'ie*) vine, often used to make baskets. It is said that the most beautiful small-leafed *maile* (MYE lee, a Native Hawaiian vine often used in *lei*) grows in the shade of the *'ie'ie* vine—just as the young *hula* students flourish under the direction of their *kumu*.

Ka Leo Kilakila (kah LEH oh KEE lah KEE lah): the majestic voice (*leo* means "voice"; *kilakila* means "majestic, strong").

K-den: "Okay, then" in Pidgin (a language that developed on Hawai'i plantations when people from different countries needed a way to communicate with each other).

keiki (KAY kee): child, children.

Kiko (KEE koh): dot, spot.

kumu (KOO moo): teacher.

lei (lay): necklace made of flowers, or sometimes of shells, beads, feathers, or other materials. *Lei* are presented to welcome visitors, to celebrate birthdays, school graduations, or other happy events, and to show appreciation and affection.

Leo Akamai (LEH oh ah kah mah ee): *leo* = voice; *akamai* = clever, smart.

Mino (MEE noh): dent, dimple.

Nani (NAH nee): beauty, beautiful.

Noelani (noh eh LAH nee): heavenly mist.

'ohe hano ihu (OH heh HAH noh EE hoo): nose flute.

pa'i (PAH ee): to slap or beat.

pū'ili (POO ee lee): a pair of bamboo sticks that are split into thin strips from one end. The other end is left whole as a grip.

'ulī'ulī (oo LEE oo LEE): a gourd rattle with seeds inside. It is attached to a handle with feathers on one end. *'Ulī'ulī* can be used singly or in pairs.

'umi (OO mee): ten.

Debi Brimmer (Auntie Kaʻie) has taught *hula* for over twenty years, and *keiki hula* for ten of those years. She has served as a teacher and a mentor most of her life: the oldest of six children, she is the mother of a son and a daughter and was active in the Girl Scouts for over fifteen years. She and Julie Coleson wrote *How Six Little Ipu Got Their Names* after Debi's young women's class got their first *ipu*.

Julie Coleson (Auntie Hiʻilani) is the assistant to the bureau chief, Office of Hawaiian Affairs, Washington, D.C. When she was growing up, she lived all over the world—including Panama, where she first learned *hula*. She has studied *hula* for over thirty years, and her daughter was one of the "new vines" for the *ipu* in the story behind *How Six Little Ipu Got Their Names*.